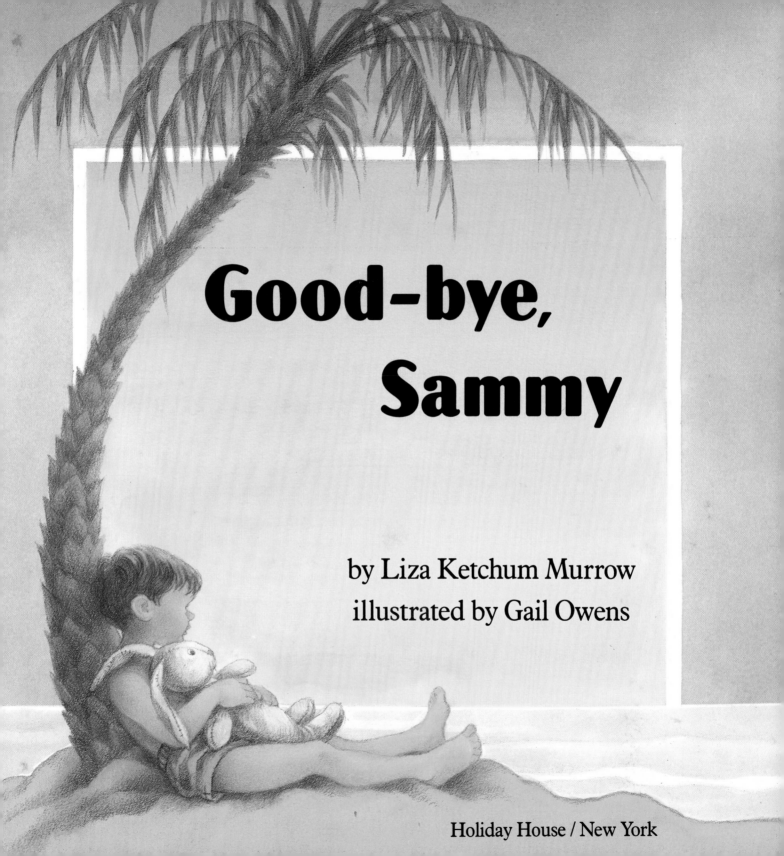

Good-bye, Sammy

by Liza Ketchum Murrow

illustrated by Gail Owens

Holiday House / New York

For Ethan, with love.
And for Mickey, wherever he may be.
L. K. M.

LIBRARY OF CONGRESS
Library of Congress Cataloging-in-Publication Data

Murrow, Liza Ketchum
Good-bye, Sammy / written by Liza Ketchum Murrow ; illustrated by
Gail Owens. — 1st ed.
p.   cm.
Summary: A child misses his lost toy rabbit even though his mother
buys him a new rabbit.
ISBN 0-8234-0726-8
[1. Rabbits—Fiction. 2. Toys—Fiction. 3. Lost and found
possessions—Fiction.] I. Owens, Gail, ill. II. Title.
PZ7.M96713Go   1989
[E]—dc19   88-17011   CIP   AC

ISBN 0-8234-0726-8

I went to Florida with my mom to see Grandma and Grandpa. Sammy came too. He's my old gray rabbit.

When we cuddled in bed the first night, Sammy and I heard the waves slap the beach.

We woke up early in the morning and ran down the
path to the seawall. The sun came up over the ocean, red
and shiny.

Every day, my mom took me swimming. Once, Sammy came too, but he was afraid of the waves. He burrowed into the sand until we could only see his tail. I dug him out. "Sammy!" I said. "You're a mess!"

I gave him a bath and pinned him on the clothesline. He was cross because the clothespins pinched his ears.

When he was dry, I let him snuggle in my arms. "Umm," I said. "You smell clean, like the wind."

Sammy and I made a fort under the sea-grape bushes. One day, we found some big paw prints in the sand. I ran to get Grandpa. He studied the tracks. "A bobcat," he said.

"Wow," I said. Sammy shivered. "Don't worry Sammy," I said. "You're safe."

But he wasn't! That same day, Grandpa's puppy chewed Sammy's nose. Sammy scurried under the table and hid, with his ears drooping over his face. I scooped him up and held him close. "Poor Sammy," I said. "That must hurt."

We made Grandma's room into a doctor's office. I gave Sammy novocaine, and then Grandma stitched him a new nose with red thread. He stayed in bed for three days.

After a week in Florida, it was time to go home.
Grandma and Grandpa took us to the airport. I made
Sammy stay in my backpack until we were on the plane.
He squeaked, because he hates being zipped up like that.

We found our seats. My mom wiped her eyes. "It's hard to say good-bye to Grandma and Grandpa," she said.

Sammy and I waved to them out the window.

The plane took off. "Hey, Sammy," I said. "Don't the cars look like matchboxes? And all those little boats are like bathtub toys." Sammy put his nose to my ear. We talked about the sailing trip we'd take when we were older.

The stewardess brought us lunch. I put Sammy on the floor so I wouldn't spill on him. After lunch, I drew pictures and my mom read to me.

Our plane was late. We hurried to meet my dad at the gate, and he tossed me up in the air. "Did you have fun?" he asked.

I told him all about our trip while we waited for our bags.

When we got home, my dad made supper. Then I felt sleepy. I went to get Sammy out of my backpack. He wasn't there!

"Mom!" I yelled. "Sammy's gone!"

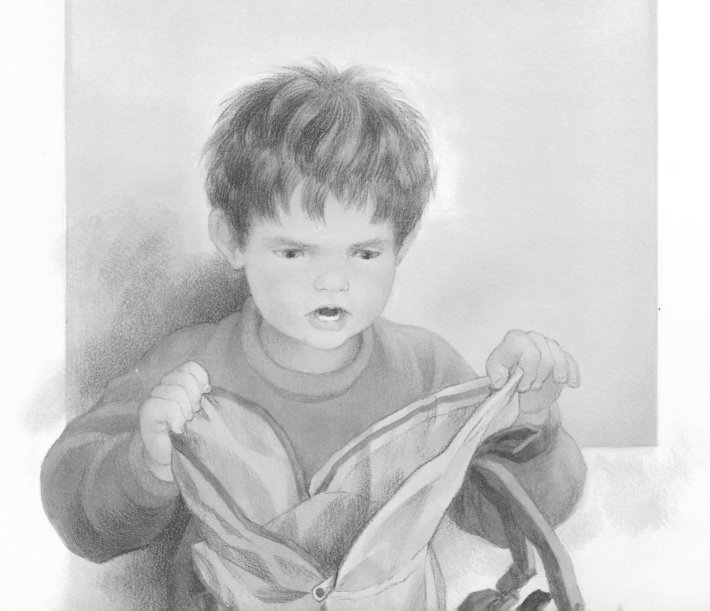

My mom came running. We looked in my pack again. We searched her carry-on bag. We checked my suitcase. No Sammy. No Sammy under my coat, or hiding in the car.

I started to cry. My mom held me. She cried too! I was
surprised. I didn't know she loved Sammy.

We looked everywhere again. Finally, I went to bed. I tried to sleep with my bear, but he didn't have Sammy's old, soft smell.

The next day, we went back to the airport. We talked to a tall woman at the ticket counter. "What did your bunny look like?" she asked.

"He used to have white fur," I said, "but it's turned gray. He has one droopy ear."

The woman typed very fast. "Your rabbit's listed in our airport computer now," she said. "We'll try to find him for you."

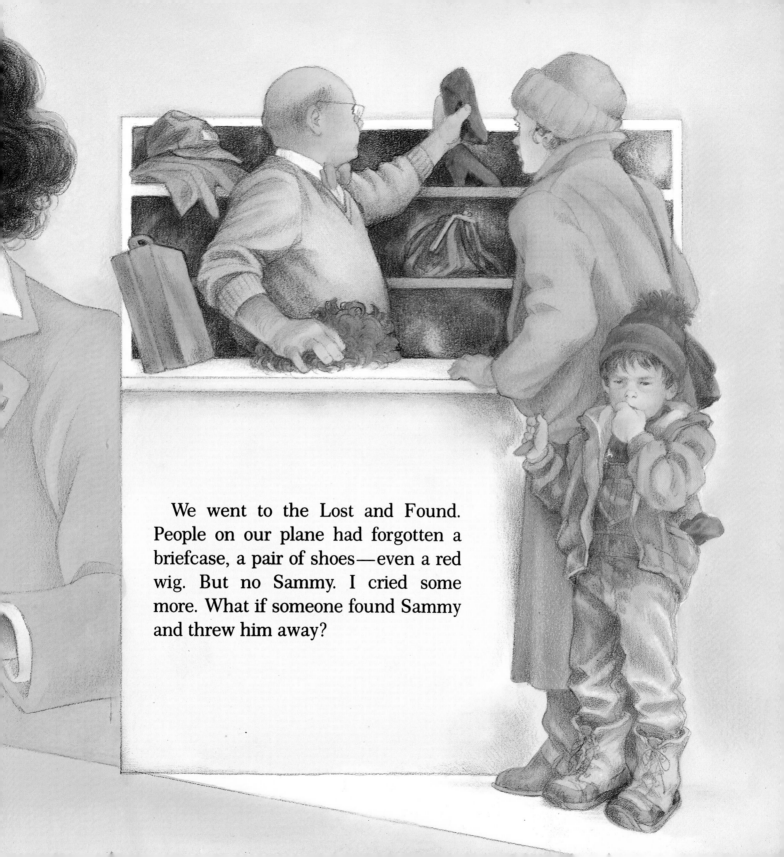

We went to the Lost and Found. People on our plane had forgotten a briefcase, a pair of shoes—even a red wig. But no Sammy. I cried some more. What if someone found Sammy and threw him away?

When we got home, I ran to my room. I looked in my old shoe box, where I keep my pictures, until I found one of Sammy. It shows him all dressed up for a party. I pinned the picture on my wall.

We waited for a week. Every day, my mom called the woman at the airport, but no one had found Sammy. At night when I went to bed, there was an empty place under my chin, where Sammy used to sleep.

One night, I dreamed about Sammy. He was sitting under a palm tree, with a pretty brown rabbit. I ran to Sammy and hugged him. He nuzzled my nose, but he wouldn't leave the other bunny.

I woke up holding my pillow. My dad heard me crying and came into my room. I told him about my dream. "I miss Sammy too," he said. He rubbed my back until I was sleepy again.

A few days later, my mom and I were in the toy store. I looked at the animal case. It was full of bears, dogs and a pig with a row of piglets snapped onto her stomach. In the corner was a rabbit just like Sammy —only bigger and fluffier.

I rushed to the front of the store and pretended to look at trucks. But then I snuck back to the case, and my mom came up next to me. "Look," I whispered. "Here's Sammy's cousin."

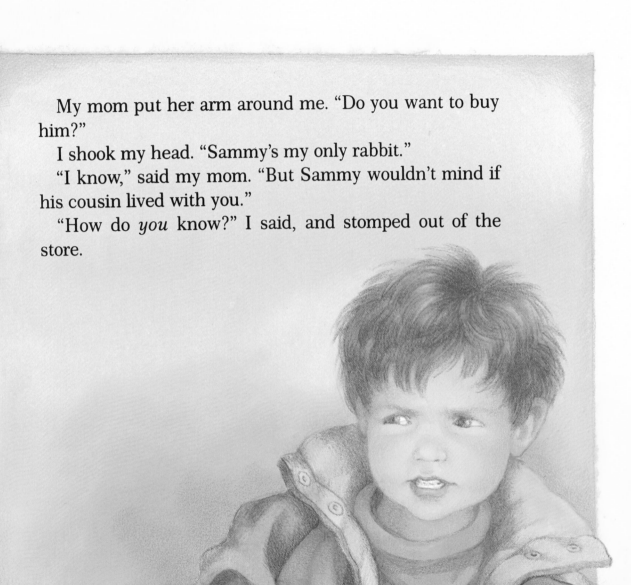

My mom put her arm around me. "Do you want to buy him?"

I shook my head. "Sammy's my only rabbit."

"I know," said my mom. "But Sammy wouldn't mind if his cousin lived with you."

"How do *you* know?" I said, and stomped out of the store.

I thought about Sammy and the other rabbit all week. One day, I found a big box in the cellar. "Just the right size for a rabbit's house," I said. I cut out a door and windows and painted a chimney on the side. Then I went to find my mom.

"I've been thinking about Sammy's cousin," I said. "Do you suppose he's lonesome in that big, glass case?"
"I bet he is," she said.

So my mom drove me to the store, and we brought the big bunny home. He wasn't cozy like Sammy. He was noisy, and he liked to bounce on my knee.

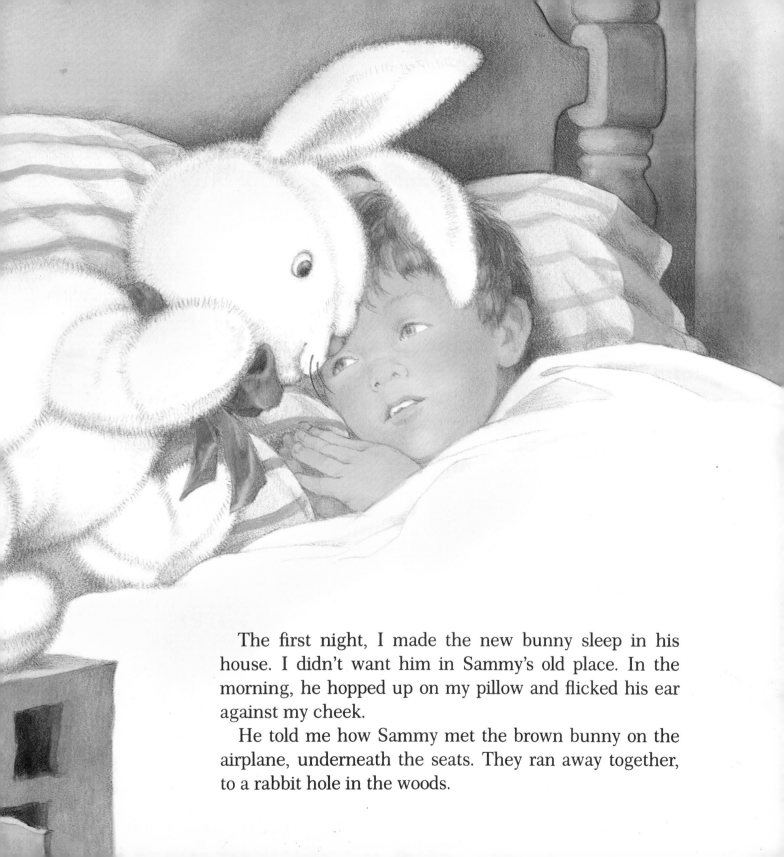

The first night, I made the new bunny sleep in his house. I didn't want him in Sammy's old place. In the morning, he hopped up on my pillow and flicked his ear against my cheek.

He told me how Sammy met the brown bunny on the airplane, underneath the seats. They ran away together, to a rabbit hole in the woods.

I was mad. "How could Sammy be happy somewhere else?" I asked my mom.

"I don't know," she said. "Maybe he fell in love, just like your dad and I did, a long time ago."

She hugged me.

My dad says the new bunny is rambunctious, so I named him Roger. Rambunctious Roger. He smells like soap, and he's always jumping around my room.

Every night before I go to sleep, I kiss Sammy's picture and tell him good night. Then I rub Roger's neck, where he likes to be scratched. I toss him in the air, until he bounces off the ceiling. We laugh together, and then we fall asleep.